Arbor Day

Lynn
Peppas

Crabtree Publishing Company

www.crabtreebooks.com

Crabtree Publishing Company

www.crabtreebooks.com

Author: Lynn Peppas

Editorial director: Kathy Middleton

Editor: Molly Aloian

Proofreader: Crystal Sikkens

Photo research: Allison Napier,
Samara Parent

Design: Samara Parent

Print coordinator: Katherine Berti

Production coordinator: Samara Parent

Prepress technician: Samara Parent

Photographs:
Dreamstime.com: page 26; © Donkeyru: page 19;
   © Mangalika: pages 28-29
© paylessimages - Fotolia.com: page 11
JBryson/iStockphoto: cover
Library of Congress: pages 6 (top), 8, 9
Shutterstock.com: title page; folio, pages 6 (bottom),
   15, 17, 23, 25, 27, 30, 31; Hung Chung Chih: page 18
Thinkstock.com: pages 4, 5, 12, 13, 14, 16
Wikipedia: ©Jon Clee: page 7; ©Jonathunder: page 10;
   ilan sharif: page 24

Library and Archives Canada Cataloguing in Publication

Peppas, Lynn
   Arbor Day / Lynn Peppas.

(Celebrations in my world)
Includes index.
Issued also in electronic format.
ISBN 978-0-7787-4085-8 (bound).--ISBN 978-0-7787-4090-2 (pbk.)

   1. Arbor Day--Juvenile literature. I. Title. II. Series:
Celebrations in my world

SD363.P47 2012   j394.262   C2012-900898-2

Library of Congress Cataloging-in-Publication Data

Peppas, Lynn.
   Arbor Day / Lynn Peppas.
   p. cm. -- (Celebrations in my world)
   Includes bibliographical references and index.
   ISBN 978-0-7787-4085-8 (reinforced library binding : alk. paper) --
ISBN 978-0-7787-4090-2 (pbk. : alk. paper) -- ISBN 978-1-4271-7844-2
(electronic pdf) -- ISBN 978-1-4271-7959-3 (electronic html)
   1. Arbor Day--Juvenile literature. I. Title.

SD363.P47 2013
633.1--dc23

                          2012004068

Crabtree Publishing Company

Printed in Canada/042012/KR20120316

www.crabtreebooks.com   1-800-387-7650

Published in Canada
Crabtree Publishing
616 Welland Ave.
St. Catharines, Ontario
L2M 5V6

Published in the United States
Crabtree Publishing
PMB 59051
350 Fifth Avenue, 59th Floor
New York, New York 10118

Published in the United Kingdom
Crabtree Publishing
Maritime House
Basin Road North, Hove
BN41 1WR

Published in Australia
Crabtree Publishing
3 Charles Street
Coburg North
VIC 3058

What is Arbor Day?

Arbor Day is a holiday. On this day, people celebrate the importance of trees. Arbor Day usually takes place in spring. People in many countries around the world celebrate Arbor Day by planting trees. They celebrate on different dates because spring occurs at different times in different countries.

Some people celebrate Arbor Day by having a picnic under a big tree.

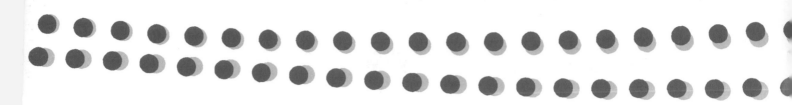

Contents

In some countries, Arbor Day is a public holiday. This means that people get the day off of work and school. In other countries, Arbor Day is an **observance**. This means that people celebrate the day, but do not get the day off. Often, in this case, schools or special groups plan tree-planting events.

- This father and son are getting ready to plant a tree on Arbor Day.

DID YOU KNOW?

Arbor is another word for tree.

5

The First Arbor Day

Arbor Day was first celebrated in the United States in the state of Nebraska. An American named Julius Sterling Morton began the celebration in 1854. He **encouraged** others to plant trees. In 1872, he planned a tree-planting holiday on April 10 of that year. Arbor Day was later changed to Morton's birthday on April 22 in honor of him.

• Nebraska is proud to be the home of Arbor Day.

DID YOU KNOW?

Over one million trees were planted in Nebraska on the first Arbor Day.

J. Sterling Morton moved to Nebraska where there were very few trees. He wanted others to help him plant trees there, so Morton held a tree-planting contest. He offered a prize to the person who planted the most trees. People in Nebraska saw the benefits to planting trees and decided to make Arbor Day a public holiday in Nebraska in 1885.

Morton's home in Nebraska is now a museum. It is surrounded by 270 varieties of trees.

Early Arbor Day Celebrations

Arbor Day in Nebraska became even more popular. In 1885, the holiday grew to include a parade. Schools planned tree-planting events for students. Students from each grade planted one tree and had to care for it throughout the year.

This tree was planted in memory of J. Sterling Morton.

After planting their trees, the students joined in the parade. Everyone marched to Nebraska City's opera house where J. Sterling Morton gave a speech. Soon after, other schools in the United States began planting trees on Arbor Day.

School children of all ages started to take part in Arbor Day celebrations.

DID YOU KNOW?

J. Sterling Morton went on to become the Governor of the Nebraska Territory!

Arbor Day Branches Out

Other Americans soon learned about Nebraska's Arbor Day and wanted to celebrate the day in cities and towns in their own states. Kansas, Tennessee, Minnesota, and Ohio were among the first few states to follow along. Soon, all Americans were celebrating Arbor Day.

● Minnesota still has a big Arbor Day celebration each year.

DID YOU KNOW?

The first Arbor Day in Connecticut was celebrated in 1887.

A man named Birdsey Grant Northrop founded Arbor Day in Connecticut. He also traveled to Europe and Australia to learn about their trees. He spent his life telling people in other countries about Arbor Day and why it was an important day to celebrate. He also wrote books about forests and about Arbor Day.

Northrop got children as far away as Japan interested in Arbor Day.

11

Amazing Trees

Trees are important parts of our **environment**. They **filter** Earth's air and keep it clean. Trees release **oxygen**, which plants and animals need to stay alive. They provide shade from the hot Sun. In winter, trees block freezing cold winds. A tree's roots also help clean soil and keep the ground from being washed away by rain.

In one year, one acre (0.4 hectares) of trees produces enough oxygen for 18 people to breath for a whole year.

People use trees to make many things we use every day. Wood from trees make paper, furniture, books, women's make-up, chewing gum, buttons, stairways, egg cartons, toothpicks, backyard play sets, houses, guitars, and thousands of others things. People cannot live without trees.

Trees create jobs for people such as those who make furniture from wood.

DID YOU KNOW?

Trees are some of the oldest living things on Earth. The bristlecone pine tree can live to be 5,000 years old!

Arbor Day in the United States

By 1920, people in every American state were celebrating Arbor Day. In 1970, President Nixon declared the last Friday in April as Arbor Day. Most states celebrate Arbor Day on this day. Some states with different growing seasons celebrate on different days. People living in the sunny state of Hawaii, for example, celebrate Arbor Day on the first Friday in November. In Alaska, the third Monday in May is Arbor Day.

The first Arbor Day in Hawaii was held on November 3, 1905, when over 3,000 trees were planted.

In the United States, people plant trees to celebrate Arbor Day. Children learn about trees at school. They write poems and make art to celebrate trees and to remember why trees are important. Some organizations hold photography contests or **scavenger hunts** on Arbor Day.

DID YOU KNOW?

*Each state has an official state tree. The state tree is commonly seen throughout the state and grows well in the state's **climate**.*

Arbor Day in Canada

Canada is a country that is made up of many **provinces**. People in different provinces celebrate Arbor Day on different dates. This is because different provinces have different climates.

DID YOU KNOW?

Canada's national Arbor Day is called Maple Leaf Day. It is held on the last Wednesday in September during National Forest Week in Canada.

In the province of Ontario, Arbor Day celebrations last for one week. The celebrations begin on the last Friday in April. People in Ontario learn about trees and plant them to celebrate the holiday. Children make posters and write speeches about the day. In Nova Scotia, people celebrate Arbor Day on the Thursday of the first full week of May.

The maple leaf, from a maple tree, is a popular symbol of Canada. It can be found on the national flag and on Canada's penny.

China's Arbor Day

People in China celebrate Arbor Day on March 12. It is a traditional tree-planting day in China. It is also a day to remember a Chinese leader named Dr. Sun Yat-sen. Yat-sen believed that planting more trees and forests would build a better environment for China.

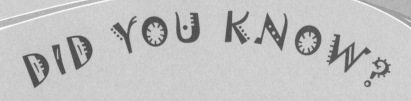

- Dr. Sun Yat-sen died on March 12, 1925. In memory of him, Arbor Day is celebrated in China on this date each year.

DID YOU KNOW?

China has planted more trees than any other country in the world.

These young students are planting trees on Arbor Day in China.

The Chinese government made tree-planting a law in 1981. This means that Chinese people from age 11 to age 60 must plant at three to five trees every year.

19

Greenery Day

Arbor Day is called Greenery Day in Japan. It is celebrated on May 4. Greenery Day is part of one week of holidays called Golden Week. Most people in Japan get the week off from school or work.

Children get time off school to enjoy nature on Greenery Day.

DID YOU KNOW?

In Japan, Greenery Day is called Midori no hi. Midori *is Japanese for* green and hi *means day.*

Japanese people plant trees on Greenery Day. The take walks in parks and gardens. Many go on hikes and enjoy the beauty of nature around them. Groups of people clean up garbage and other litter in natural areas.

- Greenery Day is a good time for students to learn more about trees and nature.

21

United Kingdom's Arbor Day

In the United Kingdom, people celebrate National Tree Week, which is a week-long tree-planting holiday. National Tree Week begins on the last Saturday in November. People plant and care for trees all week.

- The Tree Council, in the United Kingdom, helps people take care of sick trees.

The Tree Council's
National Tree Week

Every tree matters

Saturday 26th November to
Sunday 4th December 2011

Tree Council infoline: 0207 9408180
For events and ideas: www.treecouncil.org.uk

Local contact or event details:

The Tree Council is a registered charity. No 279000

DID YOU KNOW?

Every year, over half a million people take part in tree-planting events held throughout the United Kingdom.

National Tree Week is the largest annual tree celebration in the United Kingdom.

In 1973, a **government** group in the United Kingdom organized a tree-planting event. The event was so successful that The Tree Council was formed the very next year. The Tree Council began National Tree Week in 1975 and people have been celebrating ever since.

23

New Year for Trees

In Israel, people celebrate a holiday called *Tu Bishvat*, or New Year for Trees. The holiday takes place on different dates in January or February. Many people plant trees or give money to organizations so that trees can be planted on the holiday.

● These children are helping Israel's environment by planting trees on *Tu Bishvat*.

24

On New Year for Trees, Jewish people count every tree as being one year older, even if it was planted days before New Year for Trees. A tree's age is important for Jewish people because of a commandment in the Bible that says people should not eat fruit from trees that are under four years of age.

Jewish people celebrate New Year for Trees by eating dried fruits and nuts on this holiday.

DID YOU KNOW?

Tree-planting events take place in large forests in Israel on New Year for Trees. Over one million people take part in the activities.

25

Namibia's Arbor Day

Namibia is a small country in Africa. People in Namibia celebrate Arbor Day on the second Friday of October. The first Arbor Day in Namibia took place in 1991.

This woman is planting an avocado tree in Namibia.

On Arbor Day in 2011, the marula tree was Tree of the Year in Namibia. The marula tree is a fruit tree. The trees are important in Namibia because they provide people with jobs. People care for the trees and make products from the trees and its fruit.

People make marula oil from the fruit of the marula tree.

DID YOU KNOW?

Every year a Tree of the Year is chosen and planted throughout Namibia.

National Festival of Tree-planting

In India, Arbor Day is called the Tree-planting Festival. It is a week-long festival that takes place on different dates during the month of July. People in India plant millions of trees during the festival. Schoolchildren plant trees, too. They also take part in poster, artwork, and poem contests at school.

- India's Tree-planting Festival is sometimes called the Forest Festival.

DID YOU KNOW?

The Tree-planting Festival is called Van Mahotsav in India.

A government leader named K.M. Munshi started the Tree-planting Festival in 1950. He hoped that the festival would help people learn more about the importance of trees and why we need trees on Earth.

In 2011, over two million trees were planted during the Tree-planting Festival in India.

Taking Care of Trees

Every year, millions of trees are cut down. Forests are cleared to make room for new homes, stores, or factories. Trees are also cut down to make products such as paper. It is important to plant new trees and take care of young trees so there are always enough trees on Earth.

Forests of trees are cut down every day. New trees must be planted to take their place.

Special tree-planting organizations and foundations work hard to try and make sure Earth never runs out of trees. These groups organize special events and festivals to celebrate trees and all that they do for Earth. The Arbor Day Foundation in the United States is one foundation that teaches people to plant and love trees.

● You can help make Earth a better place by planting trees!

DID YOU KNOW?

You can plant a tree and help Earth. Talk to your teachers or caregivers about when Arbor Day is in your state or province and plan your own tree-planting event!

31

Glossary

climate The normal weather conditions for an area

encourage To give others the courage to try something

environment An area's natural surroundings

filter To separate materials in order to purify something or make it more healthy, such as air

government A group of people who make laws and help run a country

observance The act of following certain customs or traditions to celebrate a special time or day

oxygen A gas that cannot be seen or smelled that all living things need to survive

province A region in a country

scavenger hunt A game where participants must find items on a list in a certain amount of time

Index